The Reindeer Christmas

BY MOE PRICE

ILLUSTRATED BY ATSUKO MOROZUMI

Gulliver Books

Harcourt Brace & Company

San Diego   New York   London

Printed in Singapore

One Christmas morning, just as dawn was breaking, two
friends hurried through the forest.

"Faster, Elwin," urged Santa Claus. "The sun is coming up.
If anyone sees us, our magic will be lost forever."

The next day Santa Claus and Elwin, his chief elf, sat in front of the fire, sipping their cocoa and toasting their toes.

"Every year there are more homes to visit and more presents to deliver. There just isn't enough time anymore, Elwin," said Santa sadly. "This may be my last Christmas."

"Don't give up, Santa," said Elwin. "There must be a way." They sat in silence, thinking.

Winter was nearly over when Elwin had his wonderful idea.
"Eureka!" he cried. "That's it! That's the answer."

Plans were carefully drawn up.

But then everybody wanted to change them. Sometimes
poor Elwin could hardly hear himself speak.

Finally Elwin got everyone to agree, and soon the workshop was humming with busy, excited elves.

Santa wanted to see what was going on, but the elves would only say, "It's a secret."

At last the secret was revealed. Santa was very impressed. "Elwin," he said, "it's splendid, but . . . I can't pull this big sleigh, not even with you to help me."

Elwin held up his hand.

"An elfin wish have I but one.
I wish it once and then 'tis done.
There's magic in this gift say I,
Whoever pulls this sleigh will fly."

"But who will that be?" asked Santa. "Don't worry, Santa. We'll find someone to help us. We'll advertise."

And so they did.

The first to apply for the job was an elephant named Murray.

The takeoff was smooth.

And the landing was just perfect.

But Murray didn't get the job.

Next came Marvin the crocodile and some of his friends.

But they all had far too many teeth and looked much too hungry.

Santa Claus was very polite when he turned them down.

Rex, the leader of the huskies, knew his team could do the job. "If you want this sleigh pulled properly," he said, "you need professionals."

Certainly, the takeoff was fast, and the flight was steady.

But then Rex looked down. With a yelp of fear he tried to
climb into the sleigh with Santa. So did everyone else.

The sleigh came to a sudden stop, then fell in swoops and
circles till it sploshed into a large pond.

Through the summer many others applied.

But no one was quite right for the job.

Winter came once again and still there was no one to pull the
sleigh. Santa Claus was worried.

The day before Christmas a young reindeer knocked on
Santa's door. "One of my friends has fallen into a gorge and
broken his leg," he said. "Can you help us?"
"I'll come at once," said Santa.

"We could use the sleigh for an ambulance," said Elwin.

"That's a good idea," said Santa Claus. "But there's no one to pull it."

"We could," said the reindeer. And that is what they did.

The gorge was deep and narrow, but Santa carefully guided the sleigh to where the fallen reindeer lay.

Gently Santa and Elwin lifted him onto the soft cushions.

Then Santa whistled, and up they flew.

As soon as his friend was comfortable, the reindeer came back to see Santa Claus.

"To thank you for your kindness, we would like to pull your sleigh tonight."

"I can't think of anyone better," said Santa Claus. And so it was decided.

Now Santa Claus knew he could deliver each and every present and still be home before the sun rose on Christmas morning.

And so began a journey that would happen every year until forever.

To Richard and Vincent — A. M.

For Eleanor Doris with all the love
that ever was — M. P.

The illustrations in this book were
done in watercolor paint on Fabriano No. 5 paper.
The display type was set in Phyllis
by Thompson Type, San Diego, California.
The text type was set in Cloister
by Thompson Type, San Diego, California.
Color separations by Bright Arts, Ltd., Hong Kong
Printed and bound for Imago by Kim Hup Lee Printing Co. Pte. Ltd., Singapore
Production supervision by Warren Wallerstein and David Hough
Designed by Trina Stahl

Requests for permission to make copies
of any part of the work should be mailed to:
Permissions Department, Harcourt Brace & Company, 8th Floor,
Orlando, Florida 32887.

Library of Congress Cataloging-in-Publication Data
Price, Moe.
The reindeer Christmas/by Moe Price;
illustrated by Atsuko Morozumi. — 1st U.S. ed.
p.   cm.
"Gulliver books."
Summary: Elwin the elf helps Santa Claus find a faster
way to deliver his gifts on Christmas Eve.
ISBN 0-15-266199-9
1. Santa Claus — Juvenile fiction. [1. Santa Claus — Fiction.
2. Christmas — Fiction.]   I. Morozumi, Atsuko, 1955-   ill.
II. Title.
PZ7.P9315Re   1993
[E] — dc20   92-41076

A B C D E